# Lulu
## and the Hamster in the Night

## Praise for *Lulu and the Duck in the Park*

2013 ALSC Notable Children's Book

✩✩✩

2013 Book Links *Lasting Connection*

✩✩✩

2013 Booklist *Editors' Choice*

✩✩✩

2013 Chicago Public Library *Best of the Best*

✩✩✩

2012 Kirkus Reviews *Best Books of the Year*

✩✩✩

2013 USBBY Outstanding International Book List

✩✩✩

2013 CCBC Choice

✩✩✩

2013 ReadKiddoRead Kiddos Finalist

✩✩✩

*A Junior Library Guild selection*

········································☆········································

"McKay shows a rare ability to capture a younger audience in this involving chapter book for transitional readers. The well-structured, third-person narrative builds dramatic tension, provides comic relief of the most believable sort, and shows *plenty of heart*." —*Booklist* starred review

········································☆········································

"A *warmhearted* beginning to a new chapter book series delights from the first few sentences…What Lulu and Mellie do to protect the egg, get through class, and not outrage Mrs. Holiday is told so simply and rhythmically and so true to the girls' perfectly-logical-for-third-graders' thinking, that *it will beguile young readers completely*." —*Kirkus Reviews* starred review

········································☆········································

"McKay's pacing is *spot-on*, and the story moves briskly. Lamont's black-and-white illustrations capture the sparkle in Lulu's eyes and the warmth and fuzziness of a newly hatched duckling. The *satisfying* ending will have children awaiting the next installment in what is likely to become a hit series for fans of other plucky characters like Horrible Harry, Stink, and Junie B. Jones." —*School Library Journal* starred review

········································☆········································

"Many kids will sympathize with animal-loving Lulu, and McKay's easygoing, perceptive humor adds liveliness to the account…A lighthearted yet eventful outing, this will entice as a chaptery read-aloud as well as a read-alone." —*Bulletin of the Center for Children's Books*

········································☆········································

..................................☆..................................

"'Lulu was famous for animals,' opens this **sparkling** series launch…This offering has…**abundant humor and heart**."—*Publishers Weekly* starred review

..................................☆..................................

"McKay introduces complex characters, and animal-loving Lulu's dilemma **rings true**."—*Horn Book* starred review

..................................☆..................................

"Lulu, whose personality reminds me a lot of Ramona Quimby and Clementine, is the kind of good-hearted, bold character kids really relate to and root for." —*Secrets & Sharing Soda*

..................................☆..................................

"This is what an early chapter book should be!!" —*LiterariTea*

..................................☆..................................

# Praise for *Lulu and the Dog from the Sea*

"Whether they live with dogs or not, readers will absorb some truths about family vacations and the true care of animal companions in the company of Lulu and Mellie, who are as **utterly charming** and as completely age seven as possible."—*Kirkus Reviews*

"**Fresh as a sea breeze**, the story shows McKay's sure hand in creating characters, both human and canine. A rewarding addition to the Lulu series." —*Booklist*

"**McKay hits the nail on the head** in this beginning chapter book…This title should be a staple in any early chapter-book collection."—*School Library Journal* starred review

"Like Lulu's first outing, this is rich in the guileless and eccentric charm that is McKay's hallmark, and the details of a family sorting out the difference between a dream vacation and a real one…will ring true to many readers." —*Bulletin of the Center for Children's Books*, recommended

# Praise for *Lulu and the Cat in the Bag*

"This installment in the continuing story of Lulu, her cousin and best friend, Mellie, and her growing collection of pets delights...***It's very funny***." —*Kirkus Reviews*

☆

"McKay brings the characters to life in scenes full of warmth, wit, and perception...An ***appealing*** beginning chapter book from the ***excellent*** Lulu series." —*Booklist*

☆

"Another solid entry in this fine series" —*Horn Book*

# Praise for *Lulu and the Rabbit Next Door*

"The Lulu stories continue to hit that sweet spot: **rich with interest and humor**, tasty to read aloud, rewarding to read alone. Lamont's friendly black and white art is equally proficient at exuberant kids and nose-twitching bunnies."
—*Bulletin of the Center for Children's Books*, recommended

⋯⋯⋯⋯⋯⋯⋯⋯⋯⋯⋯⋯⋯⋯☆⋯⋯⋯⋯⋯⋯⋯⋯⋯⋯⋯⋯⋯⋯

"With its generous spot art, natural language, and **engaging** story, this beginning chapter book clearly sends a message that reading, like pet ownership, can be **a pleasure**." —*Horn Book*

Look for more books by

Hilary McKay

# Lulu
## and the Hamster in the Night

# Hilary McKay

## Illustrated by Priscilla Lamont

Albert Whitman & Company
Chicago, Illinois

Library of Congress Cataloging-in-Publication Data

McKay, Hilary.
Lulu and the hamster in the night / Hilary McKay ;
illustrated by Priscilla Lamont.
pages cm
Summary: "Seven-year-old Lulu adopts a hamster
and must keep it a secret from her grandmother
when she and her cousin Mellie spend the night"
—Provided by publisher.
[1. Hamsters—Fiction. 2. Pet adoption—Fiction.
3. Cousins—Fiction. 4. Grandmothers—Fiction.]
I. Lamont, Priscilla, illustator. II. Title.
PZ7.M4786574Luk 2015
[Fic]—dc23
2014034464

Text copyright © 2013 by Hilary McKay
Illustrations copyright © 2013 by Priscilla Lamont
First published in the UK in 2013 by Scholastic Children's Books,
an imprint of Scholastic Ltd.
Published in 2015 by Albert Whitman & Company
ISBN 978-0-8075-4842-0

Printed in China.
10  9  8  7  6  5  4  3  2  1  NP  20  19  18  17  16  15  14

For more information about Albert Whitman & Company,
visit our web site at www.albertwhitman.com.

*For Jamie Samphire*
*Wishing you lots of Happy Reading Days*
*With love from Hilary McKay*

## Chapter One

# Ratty the Hamster

Lulu was seven years old, and she was famous for animals. She was so famous for animals that people buying new pets for their children had begun to say,

*Well, if things go wrong we can always ask Lulu to take it.*

Lulu did not know they said this, and neither did her mom and dad. They might have minded, or they might not. Lulu's parents were quite famous themselves, for letting Lulu have so many pets. They said, *The more the merrier! As long as Lulu cleans up after them.* Lulu did not just clean up after them. She looked after them as if they were the most important things in the world.

And to her, they were.

At Lulu's school there was a big girl called Emma Pond. Emma Pond had a hamster. Emma Pond's hamster had a hamster wheel. The hamster ran desperately on the hamster wheel, hour after hour, day after day, week after week. It ran as if it was trying to escape. Whenever it got off the wheel it would look around as if to say "Am I still in the same place?" When it saw that it was, it tried again.

The hamster wheel made a squeaky noise that Emma Pond did not like. She used to reach through the bars with a pencil and poke the hamster off the wheel.

One day, when Emma Pond's hamster had the chance, it bit Emma Pond. This happened on a day when Emma had not been able to find a pencil and had used her finger to poke him instead. It was not a little bite; it was a big one. As big as the hamster could manage.

The next day Emma Pond came up to Lulu at school and said, "I'm getting rid of my hamster."

"Why?" asked Lulu.

"How?" asked Mellie, who was seven years old like Lulu and her best friend as well as her cousin.

Emma Pond answered them each in turn. She unpeeled a sticky bandage from her finger and showed Lulu two red holes. "That's why," she said. She told Mellie, "I'll just let it go if Lulu doesn't want it."

"Let it go where?" asked Lulu.

"Perhaps at my uncle's. He's got a big field. We let our rabbits go there."

"What happened to your rabbits?"

Emma Pond shrugged to show she didn't care. "Anyway," she said to Lulu, "my house is on the way to yours. You could stop on your way home."

"Today?" asked Lulu.

"Today, after school," said Emma Pond. "Wait at my gate. If you're not there, I'll know you don't want it."

"I want it! I want it!" said Lulu.

Right after school that day Lulu and Mellie rushed to Emma Pond's house.

"Wait!" commanded Emma when they reached the gate. Then she went in and came back carrying a small plastic cage.

Inside the cage was a heap of newspaper and hamster bedding and a hamster wheel. The rubbish heap twitched a little.

"Is it a boy or a girl?" asked Lulu.

"We never really…" began Emma Pond, and then she stopped. "It's a boy," she said. "Or if it's not, it's a girl. Obviously."

"What's its name?" asked Mellie.

Emma Pond paused. It was almost as if she didn't want to tell them. Then she said, "Ratty!"

"Ratty?" repeated Mellie.

"Ratty?" echoed Lulu. "But you said it was a hamster!"

"That's right."

"Called Ratty?"

"Are you taking him or not?" demanded Emma Pond.

"We're taking him," said Lulu.

Lulu and Mellie walked home, carrying the cage between them. With her free hand Mellie held her nose.

"I don't think Emma Pond has cleaned this cage for weeks and weeks and weeks," she said.

At Lulu's house they put the cage down on the doorstep and stretched their arms.

"We still haven't seen a hamster," said Mellie, but even as she spoke, the heap of newspaper in the cage began to move. A pink nose came out. A ginger head with bulging eyes. It yawned, showing curving orange teeth. Next Lulu and Mellie saw a ginger body with a bare patch of skin in the middle and last of all, a short hairless tail.

Then Lulu and Mellie and the ginger-colored animal all had a good stare at one another. While they were doing this, Lulu's mother came out.

"What's *that?*" she asked.

"It's a hamster," Lulu replied, and she explained about Emma Pond and Emma Pond's bitten finger and the field and the rabbits and the way Emma Pond had shrugged when Lulu had asked what happened to them.

"Well," said Lulu's mother at the end of all this, "I don't see what else you could do but bring the poor little animal home! What's its name?"

"Ratty!" said Mellie.

"Oh," said Lulu's mother. "Oh!" And then she had another look in the cage and said, "Oh. I wonder what Nan will say."

Nan was the grandmother that Lulu and Mellie shared. She was the best nan in the world. She lived on the other side of town from Lulu and Mellie, but she came to see them often. She was little and pretty

and clever and she never complained.
Not when Mellie visited and her artwork
overflowed from her bedroom, down the
stairs, through the kitchen, and across the
hall in a trail of glitter and painty splashes
and chopped-up paper. Nor when Lulu
visited and left wet animals on the sofa
and jam jars of wandering caterpillars on
the bathroom windowsill.

But Nan didn't like hamsters much.

 She didn't like the
way they moved so
quickly. She didn't
like the small sharp nails on their starfish
paws. She didn't like their raindrop eyes
or their twitchy
noses or their strange
pink tails with
the skin showing
through the fur.

Hamsters made Nan shiver.

"Perhaps we shouldn't tell Nan about
Ratty," Lulu said to her mom. "Not at first."

"First," said Lulu's mother, "before he
meets anyone, he needs a clean cage."

Ratty seemed to agree. He grabbed
the bars of his cage door with his long
orange teeth and rattled them furiously.

"I'll do it now," said Lulu, and she did,
while Mellie watched from a safe distance

and did not help. Mellie liked animals,
but not enough to scrub out their cages.
That was why she didn't have any pets.
She didn't mind playing with them,
though. She built Ratty a cardboard-box
maze to explore while Lulu scrubbed.

It had cardboard-tunnel tubes, and boxes to climb in and out of, and peanut treasure to be discovered, and Ratty seemed to enjoy it very much.

The cage was beautifully clean by the time Lulu's father came home from work. He laughed at the hamster's name and said he had once known a dog called Tiger.

"But he's not the best-looking beast in the world, is he?" Lulu's father asked.

"I'm glad he's not mine," agreed Mellie. "I don't like his teeth and I don't like his tail."

"He needs something to gnaw," Lulu said. "His teeth won't look so scary when he's worn them down a little. And soon you won't notice his tail."

"If Nan sees him she will notice his tail," said Mellie. "And she'll scream."

"She won't see him," said Lulu.

## Chapter Two

# Taming Ratty

Lulu wanted to put Ratty's cage in her bedroom, but her mom and dad did not like the idea.

"Why not the shed?" they asked. "He could make friends with the guinea pigs."

"They'd never let him," said Lulu. "Guinea pigs are only ever friends with other guinea pigs. You let me keep my old hamster in my bedroom."

"He was very small," said her mum. "And he didn't smell."

"He did," said Lulu. "He had a lovely hamster smell! It's nice having an animal living in your bedroom. Lots of people do. I've got a friend at school whose big brother has three snakes and a big lizard living in his!"

"Not really?" asked Lulu's horrified mom.

"Yes, and what will they do with them when they go on vacation?" asked Lulu. "That's what they are trying to work out!"

"Lulu, have you offered to look after three snakes and a big lizard for your friend's brother while the family goes on vacation?" demanded her father.

"Not yet," said Lulu.

"Well, don't! Do you know what snakes and big lizards eat?"

"What?"

"Hamsters!" said her father. "So you'd better choose! Which do you want? Ratty or three snakes and a big lizard, one of them with a bulge!"

"Ratty," said Lulu, and so Ratty went to live in her bedroom with no more fuss from her parents.

"I thought they said no," said Mellie when she saw him there.

"They changed their minds."

"What made them?"

"Oh, some snakes and a lizard," said Lulu.

Ratty did not become tame very quickly. Perhaps he had been poked too many times by Emma Pond's pencil for that. For days he tried to bite Lulu whenever she reached a hand toward him. He scuttled out of sight at every unexpected noise.

But he stopped running on his wheel so much. Lulu let him out so often that he didn't have to, with Lulu's bedroom to explore. Mellie's maze was there, and there were cushion mountains to climb and rugs to burrow under and delicious slices of carrots in unexpected places.

Ratty loved carrots. He would grab the carrot slices, hurry back to his cage with them, and put them safely under his bed.

Even his bed was a much cleaner bed than he had ever had before.

And his wheel didn't squeak because it had been oiled, and the bars on his cage did not make him furious because Lulu opened the door whenever she came in.

Ratty began to be pleased when Lulu came in.

He didn't hide quite so often.

He didn't try to bite quite so quickly.

"He's getting much friendlier," Lulu told Mellie proudly when Mellie came to visit one day after school.

"Never mind about Ratty," said Mellie, after one quick look. "Guess what I've been doing!"

It was easy to guess what Mellie had been doing because she was dabbled all over with pink paint and glitter.

"Making something!" said Lulu.

"A birthday present for Nan!" said Mellie, bouncing onto Lulu's bed. "Because guess what again? Her birthday's on Sunday! And guess what she's having for her birthday treat? You and me to come and stay! For all day Saturday and spending the night, and then on Sunday will be her birthday party with Mom and Dad and all of us! And that weekend the fair will be coming to the park and Nan says on Saturday we'll go!"

"But..." began Lulu.

"Don't say *but*!" ordered Mellie. "Why'd you want to say *but*? Staying at Nan's is wonderful! It's ten million times more interesting than staying at boring home!"

"I know, only what..."

"Mom's bought Nan a new pink robe for her birthday," said Mellie, "so I've been making her a pink crown to match. What if you make her a throne?"

"Yes, I could. That's a good idea. But I don't know…"

"I'll help you. It'll be easy. I can't think of anything easier to make!"

"No, listen, Mellie! That's not the problem. It's…"

"If you think our moms and dads will say no, you're wrong! They think it's a really good idea. My mom's downstairs now, talking about it to yours…"

"LISTEN, MELLIE!" shouted Lulu.

"What?"

"It's Ratty. He's just getting tame at last. I can't leave him alone for a whole weekend."

"Well, you can't take him with you!" said Mellie.

"Can't I?"

"To Nan's? Take Ratty to Nan's? Nobody would let you!"

"They might not notice. They wouldn't mind if they didn't notice."

"Nan would notice!" said Mellie.

"Not if she didn't see him."

"How could she not see him?"

"She wouldn't see him because she wouldn't know he was there. And so she wouldn't mind. Like…like…" Lulu gazed around her bedroom, searching for something that would help her explain. "Like if there was a spider living in my curtains, and you didn't know it was there. You wouldn't mind, would you?"

"Yes, I would!" said Mellie, jumping up very quickly.

"But you didn't before I said it!"

"Because I didn't know," said Mellie, beginning to walk backward to the door.

"Well, it's just the same," said Lulu. "Nan doesn't know about Ratty. She doesn't even know there is a Ratty. She's never seen him. So she doesn't mind him. And if she never does see him…"

"I've never seen a spider living in your curtains!" interrupted Mellie suddenly, and she looked suspiciously at Lulu.

"I know you haven't!" said Lulu.

"*Is* there a spider living in your curtains?
Is there?"

"Go and look if you like!" said Lulu,
rolling around on the floor laughing.

"There isn't!" said Mellie, hitting her
with teddy bears. "Ha! You're pretending!
Do you really think you can take Ratty
to Nan's without her knowing?"

"If you help."

"I always help," said Mellie. "Don't I?"

"Yes, you do," said Lulu.

"So we're all going to Nan's," said Mellie. "You and me and Ratty. So, presents! That's what I came here about. Especially the throne, because I think that's an excellent idea. Let's start it now!"

"But we have till Friday!" protested Lulu.

"You know about animals," said Mellie. "But I know about making things. I especially know how long glue takes to dry! Ages! So we'd better start now!"

Making Nan's throne took the rest of the day. It used all the rest of Mellie's pink paint and all the tinsel from the Christmas decoration box, and all the foil in Lulu's mom's kitchen and all the beads in Lulu's bead-threading kit and Mellie's mom's silver scarf. It also used all of Lulu's mom's patience and all of Mellie's mom's patience and some peacock feathers that had been hanging around for ages and the folding chair from the garden shed.

But in the end it was done, and Mellie and her mom staggered off home to bed, and Lulu went to find hers.

"Ni' night!" she murmured to her tired mom and dad and the rabbits in the hutches and the guinea pigs in the shed and the tortoise and the dogs and the parrot and Ratty.

And the spider who lived in the curtains, who nobody minded, because no one ever saw him or knew he was there.

In the night, in her dreams, Lulu worried about something. In the morning she woke up and forgot what it was.

 26

## Chapter Three

# Ratty in the Morning

On Saturday morning the packing began. Lulu and Mellie piled everything they wanted to take to Nan's in a heap by Lulu's front door, ready to be loaded into the car.

Lulu's father looked at the heap and said, "I thought you were just going to Nan's for a night."

"We are," said Lulu.

"Not an around-the-world camping trip with no shops on the way?"

"Don't be silly, Dad!" said Lulu.

"Me? Silly?" he asked. "Is this or is this not one of the hottest days of the year?"

"Mmm," said Lulu.

"Then why rain boots?"

"In case it rains and we have to go out, of course," said Lulu.

"And do you really need all those books and ten thousand felt pens?"

"They're for in case it rains and we have to stay in," explained Mellie.

"What if it gets even sunnier?" asked Lulu's father. "What about fans and sunshades and a camel or two? What if it snows, and you don't have a sled?"

Lulu and Mellie said that they didn't think it would snow and continued adding things to the pile. Roller skates and swimming things. Teddy bears. Clothes and toothbrushes. Nan's birthday cake in a tin. All the birthday presents: the robe parcel, the matching crown parcel, several other parcels, and the throne, all wrapped up.

The last thing Lulu and Mellie added was Ratty in his cage. They wrapped the cage in birthday paper and none of the grown-ups noticed. He was just one more package among many others. Lulu held him on her knee, and Mellie held the birthday cake on hers.

"All aboard?" asked Lulu's father, looking over his shoulder.

"All aboard," said Lulu.

Lulu's house was small, and so was Mellie's, but Nan's was even smaller. Nan said it had been built in the days when people didn't own so many things. Upstairs there was a miniature bathroom and two small bedrooms. Downstairs was a bit bigger because an extra bit of kitchen had been added onto the back. Lulu loved it because it was like a toy house. Mellie loved it because every room in it was perfect, bright and fresh as the inside of a shell.

Nan came running out the moment they arrived, and when she saw all the parcels and other things she said, "Oh my goodness! OH MY GOODNESS! Where are you going to put them all?"

"In our bedroom," said Lulu. "Just until tomorrow. And you can't look in case you guess what they are!"

Lulu was thinking of the throne when she said this, which still looked like a wrapped-up throne, however much paper she and Mellie taped around it. But it was useful for Ratty too. With Nan's eyes helpfully shut, he reached the little bedroom that Lulu and Mellie were to share quite easily. Lulu and Mellie dumped him on Lulu's bed and surrounded him with parcels.

"You'd never guess he was there!" said Mellie, bouncing a bit.

"Shush!" said Lulu.

When at last the car was unloaded, Lulu's dad said good-bye and told Nan how good he hoped they would be. And Nan said that she knew they would be as good as gold, because they always had been, right from the moment they were born.

"Oh yes," said Lulu's dad. "I don't know why I keep forgetting that."

Then he hugged everyone very quickly and hurried away.

Lulu and Mellie and Nan waved from the gate until he was gone, and then Lulu remembered Ratty upstairs, still in his birthday parcel.

"Shall we unpack now?" she asked.

"Later," said Nan. "First we will have drinks by the pool!"

"What pool?" asked Lulu and Mellie together.

"The one by the orange and lemon tree," said Nan, and she led them around the corner of her very small house, into her very small garden, and pointed proudly.

There was Nan's very small tree and under it was a beautiful blue paddling pool with flowers floating in the water.

"Oh, Nan!" exclaimed Lulu and Mellie, their hot shoes already kicked off, their feet already dabbling.

"And look at my tree!" said Nan.

The little tree was transformed. Dangling from its branches were oranges and lemons, grapes and bananas and rainbow-colored candle lanterns, waiting to be lit. Large bright paper butterflies balanced on the branches. Mellie spied a pineapple and Lulu, who all her life had wanted to climb a coconut tree and pick a real coconut, now found that she could.

"It's a jungle tree!" said Mellie. "You should have brought your parrot, Lulu, instead of just that ha..."

*Splash!*

Lulu had climbed into the tree to have a closer look at the coconut. Now Mellie was suddenly much wetter and the coconut was bobbing in the pool. And on the far side of the tree, where Nan had spread rugs and cushions, three furry golden shapes were suddenly awake. Six bright green eyes were staring indignantly at the coconut.

They belonged to Marigold, Nan's enormous golden cat, and Dandy and Daisy, her two fat kittens.

All at once Lulu remembered what it was that she had worried about in her dreams.

Right out loud, Mellie exclaimed, "Lulu! We forgot about the cats! They're good cats, though, aren't they, Nan? They don't go around killing things like some cats do."

"Certainly not!" said Nan.

"Not even rats or mouses or hamsters or things?"

"Mice!" said Nan. "Not mouses! No, not even butterflies!"

Lulu was so afraid of what Mellie would say next that she slid down the tree, put a cushion on Mellie's head, sat on it, and changed the subject.

"What made you think of an orange and lemon tree, Nan?"

"Oh," said Nan. "First I wished I had an orange tree, and then I thought I'd make an orange tree! And then I thought, why just oranges? So I added the lemons and everything else. I thought you could help yourselves to fruit just as easily from the tree as you could from the fruit bowl."

"*Can* we help ourselves?" asked Mellie, wriggling out from beneath the cushion and Lulu.

"Of course. Shall I show you how to open up the coconut?"

But Lulu and Mellie would not hear of that. There was only one coconut and they thought it would be a waste to eat it so soon.

"Let's hang it back up again," said Lulu.

Nan had hung the coconut by a string tied around its middle. It was not an easy job to tie the string without it slipping. Over and over the coconut splashed down into the paddling pool and either Lulu or Mellie had to climb the tree and try again. They enjoyed this very much, but the cats did not. Every time the coconut fell again, they looked more disapproving and moved a little farther away.

It was amazing how quickly the morning went by. Paddling and coconut hanging. Learning how to make paper-plate

butterflies. Bubble-blowing
from the top of the
tree. They had to
take turns to do
this because the
tree was
so small.

"Do the
cats like the
bubbles?" called
Mellie when it
was her turn
to climb.

Lulu looked
around. Where
were the cats?

"Gone to get away from the splashes,"
guessed Mellie.

"Gone to find some shade," suggested

Nan. "It's getting hotter and hotter. I've opened all the doors and windows to get a breeze through the house."

"All the doors!" repeated Lulu.

"Don't worry, I didn't look when I opened yours," said Nan.

That didn't stop Lulu worrying. She rushed upstairs and sure enough, there were Nan's three cats.

Nan's cats were stay-at-home cats. It was true that they never went hunting. They liked sofas and cushions and large meals and sunshine. They had their own cat brushes and their own cat china bowls and at Christmastime they had their own cat Christmas presents under the Christmas tree.

Lovely smelly cat treats, that's what the cats had had, wrapped in Christmas paper. It was Lulu who had wrapped those parcels, and Lulu who had shown the three cats how to unwrap them, ripping the paper with their claws.

Nan's cats had not forgotten. And now they had found a parcel larger and smellier and more exciting than anything they had unwrapped at Christmas.

When Lulu came into the bedroom, there they were, eagerly unwrapping the parcel that was Ratty in his cage.

Mellie had followed Lulu when she ran. Now she looked around the little room, which seemed absolutely bulging with parcels, and said, "Weren't they clever to find the right one!"

"Clever!" said Lulu. "Help me shoo them away! Look at poor Ratty!"

Ratty was not happy. His eyes were bulging and his ears were flat. He trembled

at the furry faces so close to his. His pink
tail twitched in fear. Lulu picked up the
whole cage and hugged it, while Mellie
shooed the cats.

The cats did not want to be shooed.
They looped around Mellie's legs and
jumped among the jumble of things in
the room and tried very hard to get back
to their parcel.

"What is the matter?" called Nan up the stairs.

"Nothing!" called Mellie as she scooped up a kitten. "Only the cats!" She grabbed the other.

With a kitten under each arm, Mellie chased Marigold out of the room and pulled the door shut behind her. Lulu heard her panting. She heard the double thud of kittens jumping to the floor. She heard Nan ask, "Can I help?"

"No, no, no!" said Mellie. "You can't! Because it's a…a…"

"Surprise?" suggested Nan. "Don't tell me anymore! What's Lulu doing?"

"She's sorting it out," said Mellie.

Sorting out Ratty took a long time. A lot of patient talking. A great many comforting carrot slices. Ages before he would let

Lulu pick him up and carry him around the room to show him that there was nothing to be afraid of anymore. And when Lulu finally left him and opened the door, there were all the cats on the little landing, waiting for the moment when they could rush back to their present.

"No, no, no!" Lulu told them, hurrying them down the stairs and into the kitchen, where Mellie and Nan were making lunch.

"Now, Lulu," said Nan, kindly not saying anything about how long she had been, "where shall we have lunch? Inside or outside?"

"Outside, please," said Lulu at once. "With the cats! Come on, cats!"

Nan and Mellie laughed when Lulu said that, because the cats came at once. They followed after Lulu in a prowly golden parade. They followed her outside with the

lunch things and in again to help carry
drinks and up the tree to pick bananas and
back to the kitchen for ice cream.

They seemed to have decided not to
let her out of their sight. The only place
they wouldn't follow her was into the
paddling pool. They sat around the edge
glaring, waiting till she came out.

Sooner or later, thought the cats, Lulu
would lead them back to their present.

"They are bewitched!" said Nan.

"Can we take them with us?" asked Lulu.

"What?" asked Nan, astonished. "Cats?
To the fair? I don't think so, Lulu!"

"What will they do, then, while we
are away?"

"Just snooze, I suppose."

"Inside?"

"Oh yes, don't worry, they won't be
locked out!"

"They can't open doors, can they, Nan?" asked Mellie.

"They don't need to," said Nan cheerfully. "They can walk through walls!"

"Not really?" asked Mellie.

"No, of course not really!" said Nan, laughing. "Now, off you go and get ready if you want to go out today!"

Lulu and Mellie went.

The cats followed. Through the house. Up the stairs.

"Sorry, cats," said Lulu as she closed the bedroom door on them.

The cats were sorry too.

Three sets of urgent paws began clawing at the door.

"It's a scary sound," said Lulu. "If you didn't know what it was, wouldn't it be awful?"

"Or even if you thought you did," said Mellie, "but were wrong! You might think, 'Oh, I'll just let Nan's cats in,' and open the door, and there would be a great big grizzly bear! Or a lion or a tiger or one of those T. rexes!"

Mellie obviously liked the idea of such a frightening surprise and usually Lulu would have felt the same. But having Ratty to take care of made everything different.

"Think how it must sound to him!" she said. "What if the cats do it all afternoon? There'll be no one here to rescue him. Perhaps I'd better not go!"

"You can't not go!" said Mellie at once. "This is Nan's treat! It would spoil it. You'll just have to put him somewhere safe…"

She looked around the little room, crowded with packing and presents. Lulu looked too. And Lulu said, "The roof!"

Long ago, an extra bit of house had been built onto Nan's kitchen. It stuck out a little way into her garden and it had a flat roof. The flat roof was right under Lulu and Mellie's bedroom window. It looked like a patch of gravelly stones, with a little wall around the edge.

At first Nan had thought it would be a good place to grow flowers and she had put plant pots up there. But she had soon grown tired of climbing in and out of the window to water them. Now there was only one plant left, a pink rose that grew all around the window. Nan could water that without climbing. She just had to lean out of the window and she could reach its tub.

There were not many things that Lulu and Mellie were not allowed to do at Nan's house. They were allowed to dress up in her beads and hats and dig for treasure in her garden. They were allowed to cook in her kitchen and slide down her banister. They had made a Harry Potter house in the cupboard under her stairs. Once Mellie had played Titanic in her bathroom. Once Lulu had tucked up a hedgehog on the sofa.

But they were not allowed to play on the roof.

*Scratch! Scratch! Scratch!* went the bears or the lions or the tigers or the T. rex or perhaps the cats at the door.

"We aren't allowed to play on the roof," said Mellie as Lulu opened the window.

"This isn't playing," said Lulu, and she leaned out and lowered Ratty's cage onto the gravelly flatness outside.

And there he was. He had blue sky above and cool shade all around him. He had roses to smell and lovely fresh air. And when the window was closed he was quite safe.

 49

"And no one will know he is there!"
said Lulu triumphantly.

Even looking up from the garden she could not see his cage. The little wall hid it.

Ratty was quite safe from the cats, and Nan was quite safe from Ratty.

Then, one on each side of Nan, taking care of her because it was her birthday treat, Lulu and Mellie went to the fair in the park.

*Chapter Four*

# Ratty on the Roof

There never was a better person to take to a fair than Nan. She never said, as Lulu's and Mellie's parents so often did, "Once is enough!" or "Wait till you're older!" She never said, "You're not eating that!"

Once was not enough for Mellie on the Sky Wheel or Lulu on the carousel or Nan on the bumper cars. They tried them all twice and many other things too. And they ate cotton candy and hot dogs and terrible sticky rock candy. Also, by rolling balls and throwing hoops and catching ducks, they succeeded in winning a giant blow-up parrot, a long purple scarf made from feathers, a green balloon that rattled like thunder, and a solar-powered glow-in-the-dark plastic garden gnome.

"Extra birthday presents for you!" said Lulu to Nan.

Then they wound the feather scarf around Nan's neck, and Lulu took the parrot and the balloon, and Mellie took the gnome in one hand and Nan's hand in the other, and they walked home very slowly together.

"Did you have a nice time, Nan?" asked Mellie.

"I had a wonderful time," said Nan. "I haven't laughed so much for years and years and years. But I shall be very glad to sit down!"

The cats were pleased to see them come home. They mewed and curled around their legs, explaining how hungry they were.

"Wait five more minutes," Nan told them, collapsing on the sofa.

In less than five minutes Lulu and Mellie heard the first gentle snore.

Very quietly Lulu and Mellie fed the cats and put away the prizes. Then Mellie got out supper things in the kitchen and Lulu went upstairs to see how Ratty had enjoyed the roof. She found him chewing at the bars, the way he did when he could not endure his cage any longer.

Lulu looked at the crowded bedroom. Then she looked at the roof, all airy and clear, with the little wall around the edge. Then she did something she had never done before. She climbed out of the window.

And she opened Ratty's door.

Mellie said, "Lulu! We're *not* allowed to play on the roof!"

"I'm not playing," said Lulu. "I'm exercising Ratty. He's having a lovely time. Look!"

☆ 56 ☆

Ratty did look happy. Lulu had put her quilt onto the roof and arranged it into tunnels. He was diving in and out, exploring them, and when he wasn't doing that, he was collecting rose petals that had fallen from the tub of pink roses, climbing through the open door of his cage and tucking them into his bed.

Mellie looked for a while and then she asked, "Is it nice out there?"

"Lovely," said Lulu, stretched out on her back. "There's loads and loads of sky."

Mellie climbed out of the window too. She stretched out beside Lulu.

"This isn't playing," she said. "It's just lying down."

"Yes," agreed Lulu.

"The cats are looking for you out in the garden. Nan's awake. She said to tell you there are penguins on TV. You go and watch them and I'll stay here with Ratty."

"Don't you want to watch the penguins?"

Mellie shook her head. She had endured many penguin programs and once a whole film.

"I know what it will be like," she said, yawning. "The TV people will say: 'These are penguins. They live a very hard life'. And the penguins will stand around on the ice. For ages and ages and ages! Anyway, you're missing them. You'd better hurry up before Nan wonders where you are."

So Lulu scrambled back through the window and downstairs to Nan. Nan laughed when Lulu told her what Mellie had said about penguins.

"What's Mellie doing?" she asked.

"Nothing," said Lulu. "Well, looking at the sky and yawning!"

"Everyone's tired," said Nan. "After these penguins I think supper, then bed."

"Then it'll be your birthday," said Lulu. "Are you excited about tomorrow, Nan?"

"I'm always excited about tomorrow," said Nan. "You just never know what will happen, do you?"

The penguins caught fish. They stood around on ice. Lulu watched, fascinated. The TV people explained what a hard life it was. Mellie appeared in the doorway.

"I told you so," she said. "All penguin programs are exactly the same!"

"Mellie!" exclaimed Lulu. "I thought you were looking after...looking at...the sky!"

"I've looked at it," said Mellie. "It went all rosy." Behind Nan's back, Mellie puffed out her

cheeks and scrabbled invisible rose petals into her mouth with her paws. "Then it

went very quiet…" Mellie's head nodded forward, eyes closed, limp-pawed, a hamster asleep.

"So I came down," finished Mellie and stopped being a hamster and started trying to stand on her head instead.

The penguins finished. A new show started about criminal minds.

"No, thank you!" said Nan. "No criminal minds here!" And she switched off the TV so that the screen became blank except for Mellie's reflection.

"I shut the door," said Mellie from upside down.

Lulu and Nan sighed with relief.

After supper Nan sent the girls upstairs.

"Baths, pajamas, bed!" she said.

The cats followed after them. They prowled around the bedroom, sniffing the wrapped-up parcels, searching for their present. But the window was shut and they could not find it anywhere. They marched into the bathroom and looked at Lulu with such round indignant faces that the girls could not stop laughing.

"The cats think you ate it!" said Mellie.

"Cats! Cats! Cats!" called Nan. "Bring them down, girls! I'll shut them in the kitchen or they'll wander the house all night."

Lulu and Mellie took the cats down to the kitchen and tucked them into their basket. "Good night!" they said, hugging first the cats and then Nan. "Thank you for the fair and the park and the tree and the pool!" They gave Nan extra hugs because she had been such a very good nan. "And because it is almost your birthday," added Mellie.

"You won't come into our room tonight, will you?" asked Lulu anxiously.

"Goodness, no!" said Nan. "I know it is full of secrets!"

Lulu and Mellie looked guiltily up at her.

"Bed!" said Nan. "Bed for all of us!" And she chased them up the stairs and followed behind.

As soon as Lulu and Mellie were in their room and the door was safely closed, Lulu went across to the window.

"I won't take a minute!" she told Mellie. "You stay inside and I'll pass Ratty up to you."

She was out of the window before
Mellie could say, "Why not leave him
there all night?" Lulu bent to pick up
the cage. Mellie heard a small squeak.

The squeak was
not Ratty. It
was Lulu.

"Mellie! Mellie! Mellie!" squeaked Lulu.
"You didn't shut the door!"

"I did!" said Mellie indignantly, and
Lulu saw her glance over her shoulder
as she spoke, as if to make sure she had
shut it again.

"Not the bedroom door, the cage door!"

"I…" began Mellie, and then she said, "Oh. OH! But he was asleep!"

"He's not now." Lulu's hand searched the cage, sifting through hamster bedding and rose petals with her fingers. "He's gone."

"There's nowhere for him to go," said Mellie, and she looked around the little roof space, empty except for the cage, dusky in the corners, bare right up to the little walls…

"Could he have climbed down the walls?" Mellie asked, and she made a moaning sound at the thought.

Lulu was already leaning over the walls, peering into the shadows at the base, hoping not to see a bundle of orange fur.

"Oh, oh, oh," said Mellie unhappily, and then in a completely different voice, "Oh! There he is!"

Ratty had
not fallen
over the wall.
He was climbing
the rose bush,
or rather the trellis
that held the rose bush
against the house. He was
almost at the top. Nearly at the place
where the roof tiles sloped down to reach
the wall.

"Don't make him jump!" begged Lulu.
"He might get frightened and fall."

But Ratty did not look frightened. He
looked busy and happy.

He looked like he had been climbing
houses all of his life.

"He'll have to turn around and come
back when he reaches the top," whispered
Lulu, but Ratty did not turn around. He

reached the top, examined the edge of the roof, and vanished.

Lulu and Mellie waited and waited and waited.

Nothing happened.

"Stupid hamster," growled Mellie.

"Stupid you, not shutting the door!"

"Stupid you, bringing him! And now where is he?"

Lulu felt the rose trellis against the wall. It wasn't very strong, but at least it didn't wobble. She looked at the rose, and wished it wasn't prickly.

"Don't!" said Mellie. "What if you fell?"

"I'd only fall on the flat roof," said Lulu. "Anyway, I won't."

All the same, she climbed the trellis very carefully, getting rather scratched. It was not high. Two steps and she had reached the top, the place where Ratty

had disappeared. Lulu reached out a hand
and felt.

"There's a hole!" she whispered down
to Mellie.

"A hole in the roof?"

"Yes. Underneath. Just a little one. It must go into the attic."

"Nan doesn't have an attic."

"I mean the empty space in the roof over the bedroom ceilings. Dad showed me ours once. It's all dusty and there's a water tank and it's dark and there's cobwebs."

"Squeeze your hand through the hole and see if you can touch Ratty," suggested Mellie.

Lulu tried, but she couldn't.

"We'll have to think of another way of getting him back," she said as she carefully climbed back down the trellis.

"What does he like best?"

"Carrots," said Lulu. "He loves carrots. If you give him carrots he takes them to bed."

"Do you think if we put a carrot in the hole at the top of the trellis he might smell it and come and get it?"

"He might," said Lulu. "Perhaps we could put a trail of carrot pieces leading down to his cage. Only I don't have any carrots left. Ratty ate it all this afternoon. Maybe Nan has some."

"I'll go and see," said Mellie, and she ducked back into the bedroom again. Then she paused, looking up at the ceiling.

"Lulu! Lulu!"

"What?"

"Come and listen! I can hear him!"

"I'll go and look for a carrot," said Mellie and tiptoed out of the room. Lulu heard her feet on the stairs, the murmur of her voice as she spoke to the cats, the thud of the fridge, opening and closing, and then she was coming back up the stairs again. And then there was Nan's voice, at her own bedroom door.

"Mellie!"

"Hello, Nan! I just wanted a carrot!"

"A carrot!"

"Carrots are healthy!" said Lulu, appearing suddenly beside Mellie.

Nan had very sparkly eyes sometimes. They sparkled now at Lulu. She said, "So they are! Well. Eat up your carrot and go to sleep. It's very late."

"How late?" asked Lulu.

"It's after half past ten."

"Less than an hour and a half to your birthday, then," said Lulu. "Oh…"

Patter, patter, patter, went the footsteps overhead.

Lulu gazed at Mellie in alarm, and then, to everyone's surprise, she began to sing. She sang much louder than she usually did, her eyes fixed on Nan.

"*Happy-birthday-in-an-hour-and-a-half to you!* (Join in, Mellie!)"

"*Happy-birthday-in-an-hour-and-a-half to you!*" Mellie also sang very noisily, glancing up at the ceiling.

"*Happy-birthday-in-an-hour-and-a-half, dear Na-an!*" they chorused anxiously.

"*Happy-birthday-in-an-hour-and-a-half to you!*"

Lulu and Mellie stopped. And listened. Nan, who had suddenly doubled up with laughter, hugged them.

And then Lulu and Mellie scurried back to their room and they sat on their beds in the dark and they whispered.

"I suddenly heard him!"

"I guessed you did!"

"Good thing I thought of 'Happy birthday'!"

"Yes, but what now?"

They listened and listened and listened.

They heard the breeze in the wind chimes that hung from the orange and lemon tree.

They heard tired Nan snoring her ladylike snores.

They heard, just once and far away, the raindrop patter of Ratty's feet on the plaster ceiling.

They heard a sudden clawing.

It might have been bears. It might have been tigers. It might have been lions or one of those T. rexes.

"The cats!" said Lulu.

Down in the kitchen, the cats were scratching at a wall.

*Snore*, went Nan again, as Lulu and Mellie tiptoed past her bedroom door.

The cats hardly looked at Lulu and Mellie as they crept into the kitchen. They were up on the cupboard, glaring at the wall.

Their golden ears were pricked into
flags. They tilted their heads to listen.
Then they scrabbled at the wall with
their twelve golden paws.

They were not at all pleased when
Lulu and Mellie scooped them up around

their furry middles, carried them to the living room, dumped them on the sofa, and closed the door.

"Now listen!" said Lulu to Mellie.

They listened and sure enough they heard Ratty, climbing around on the other side of the wall.

"He must have climbed right down from the roof!" whispered Mellie.

Lulu and Mellie unlocked the back door and tiptoed into the garden and were very surprised not to see Ratty clinging to the wall.

"But we heard him!" said Lulu, very puzzled, and she stepped back into the kitchen to listen. Once again, there was Ratty, plain to be heard, climbing around.

But outside, no Ratty. Nothing.

So Mellie stayed inside and Lulu found a flashlight and went outside and they left the door open and Mellie called directions. "He's right beside the window! Now he's a bit lower! He's halfway down now, between the window and the floor!"

Lulu peered, more and more puzzled, at the outside wall of Nan's little kitchen. Then suddenly she understood. Walls were not one brick thick, like Lego house walls. They were two bricks thick. There was an inside wall and an outside wall, with a gap in between.

And in the gap in between was Ratty.

When Lulu understood this she rushed inside and told Mellie they must call the fire department to come and knock down the house.

"The whole house?" asked Mellie, dreadfully shocked.

"Only the back half," said Lulu.

"That's a lot of house, though," said Mellie, and she picked up the phone and held it behind her back to stop Lulu from arranging anything reckless.

"It's the wrong thing to do!" said Mellie. "Especially on Nan's birthday! Just listen to Ratty! There he is again! Right under the window."

They both went outside again, and shone the flashlight at the wall, and while they were there Lulu noticed something.

Not all the bricks were the same. One, low down, almost on the ground, was not solid. It was brick colored. It was made out of brick. But it looked like a little grating. A little grating, an air brick, with little square holes like windows, opening into the wall.

Lulu lay down on her stomach and shone her flashlight through the holes.

There, on the other side, was Ratty.

For a moment it seemed to Lulu and Mellie that all their problems were solved. There was Ratty. They had found him. And Nan was still asleep in bed.

"All we have to do," said Lulu, "is to make those little holes big enough for Ratty to squeeze out."

"Easy peasy!" said Mellie at once.

They fetched from the kitchen the tin opener and a screwdriver and they set to work.

After a while they went back for the potato peeler and some spoons.

Small flakes of air brick broke away in thin sharp splinters.

Mellie crept upstairs and brought down their swimming goggles.

Ratty scurried around on the other side of the wall. He was very happy. He had never had any adventures living with Emma Pond.

Time passed.

The stars swung around the sky.

Lulu and Mellie's knees began to ache.

"What we need," said Lulu, "is a very big hammer."

For as long as Lulu and Mellie could remember, Nan had lived alone in her little bright house. But once there had been a big, quiet Granddad living there too. He had liked making things and he had owned a shed full of tools. It was still there, right at the end of the garden, beyond the orange and lemon tree.

Mellie took the flashlight and visited Granddad's shed, and she came back with a very big hammer indeed.

"Perfect!" said Lulu, and she seized it from Mellie, swung it mightily back into the air, and walloped the air brick with the most tremendous crash.

"Careful!" cried Mellie, forgetting to be quiet.

"I am being careful!" said Lulu and did it again. She was about to swing it a third time when Nan appeared.

"Lulu! Mellie!" exclaimed Nan. "*It's one o'clock in the morning!*"

That surprised them.

"Wow! One o'clock!" said Mellie, and Lulu said brightly, "Happy birthday, Nan!'

"Yes, yes! Happy birthday, Nan!" agreed Mellie.

"Happy birthday!" said Nan indignantly. "HAPPY BIRTHDAY! Never mind 'Happy birthday'! What in the world are you doing?"

Lulu looked at Mellie.

Mellie looked at Lulu.

"We've lost something in the wall," said Lulu at last.

"Something?" repeated Nan.

"Yes," said Mellie, "and we didn't want to call the fire department, not on your birthday."

"*The fire department?*"

"To knock down your house!"

"Really only the back half," put in Lulu soothingly.

"So," continued Mellie, "we thought we would just bang a hole in this holey brick…"

"That one at the bottom with gaps in it," said Lulu.

"…and let it out," said Mellie.

"*Get* it out!" corrected Lulu. "Not let, get! If it's still there."

She lay down again with the flashlight to check. "Poor little thing!" said Lulu.

"Oh!" said Nan.

"Ah!" said Nan.

"I see!" said Nan, and she looked down at Lulu and nodded.

Lulu didn't notice. She was down on her stomach again, shining the flashlight. At first there was nothing, but then ginger fur appeared. An inquisitive dark eye glinted silver in the flashlight.

 83

"Is he still there?" asked Mellie, getting down to join her.

"Still there," said Lulu, sighing with relief. "I think perhaps he goes away when we bang and then comes back when the flashlight is shining."

Then they both rolled over and looked guiltily at Nan.

There was a small silence while Nan looked back at them.

"Well," she said at last. "We'd better take turns with the hammer!"

*Chapter Five*

# Ratty in the Morning

Deep in the night, in Nan's little garden, Lulu and Mellie and Nan took turns, sharing the hammer and the swimming goggles. Every now and then they would pause their banging and Lulu would lie down with the flashlight to check that the lost thing was still there.

Once, when Mellie was hammering, Lulu thought she heard something. Then she thought she hadn't, because who would ever telephone in the middle of the night.

Nan was having her turn when the police cars arrived.

Two of them, blue lights flashing.

As well as four large policemen with flashlights so bright they put out the stars.

Lulu and Mellie ran one each side of Nan, and they held her tight.

"Don't you worry!" Lulu told her. "We'll look after you! We'll tell them it's your birthday!"

That didn't need to be done. They were very nice policemen, not at all as scary as they looked.

They were very polite too. They said, "Would you mind telling us what is going on?"

Lulu looked at Mellie.

They both looked at Nan.

Then they looked at the waiting policemen and Mellie asked, "Can we whisper?"

"Can they whisper?" the largest policeman asked Nan, and Nan nodded yes.

So Lulu and Mellie took the largest policeman down to the orange and lemon tree and they explained everything that had happened. They began with Emma Pond and they ended with the hammer. And while they were doing it, Nan made everyone cups of tea.

The policemen took their cups of tea under the orange and lemon tree and they stood in a circle around the paddling pool and Lulu and Mellie's policeman told the others all that he had discovered. He was very careful to whisper.

Then all the policemen came back smiling and told Nan and Lulu and Mellie how pleased they were to find that they didn't have to rescue a poor old lady from desperate burglars. That was what they had expected, when Nan's neighbor had called them to say that his next-door neighbor would not answer her telephone and the bangs were terrible and peering from his window he could see three shadowy criminals knocking down the walls.

Then three of the policemen went away in case they were needed for any other emergencies that night.

But the largest policeman stayed. He whispered to Lulu and Mellie that he had three children at home and three hamsters to match, and he knew what to do when hamsters became lost things.

First, with bangs ten times louder than any that Lulu or Mellie or Nan had made, he knocked out the air brick.

Next, using a bucket, two clothes pegs, a long dangling scarf, something soft to land on, and Mellie's carrot, sliced up, he made a lost-thing catcher. He fixed the scarf to the bucket with the clothes pegs at one end. He dangled the other end in the air-brick hole.

"That makes a ladder to the top of the bucket," he said.

Next he put a trail of carrot slices all the way up the scarf-ladder. He put more carrot inside the bucket, on top of a folded kitchen towel. Then he explained:

"Whatever you have lost will smell the carrot, climb the scarf, tumble in the bucket, land safely on the towel and there you go!" he told them. "All you have to do is wait. Trust me! I'm a policeman!"

Then he went away too.

"Well," said Nan, "this is the most exciting birthday I've had for years! And now we'd better make ourselves comfortable while we wait!"

Lulu and Mellie fetched rugs and cushions for themselves, but they did not fetch rugs and cushions for Nan. They fetched her crown and her throne, because it was her birthday.

When Nan saw her crown and throne she said Lulu and Mellie were, as she had always supposed, the very best girls in the world. Whatever they had lost in the walls.

And then she settled down on her throne in the garden, and Lulu and Mellie curled up on their cushions.

And, although they did not mean to, one by one they fell asleep.

But Ratty did not.

Ratty stayed awake.

Ratty was cleverer than the policeman's children's hamsters.

He was cleverer than the policeman too. He found his carrot slices.

One by one he picked them up, carried them down the scarf, through the hole in the air brick, up the walls, across the roof, down the rose trellis and into his cage, where he put them away under his bed.

He was very careful not to fall in the bucket.

When he had collected all his carrot slices he went to bed.

On the roof.

Lulu found him the next morning, still fast asleep. The cats showed her where he was. The cats always knew.

Lulu picked him up, cage as well, and carried him downstairs. Mellie was awake now, but Nan was not.

*Snore!* went Nan, very gently and quietly, her crown tipping sideways, asleep on her throne.

"Look!" whispered Lulu, and Mellie said, "Wow!"

Later that day the parents arrived and they exploded at once into questions.

"What *have* you been up to?"

"What's that hole in the wall?"

"Why are you yawning?"

"And *have* you been good?"

"They've been as good as gold," said Nan, overhearing. "All of them perfect! All three!"

"Three?" asked Mellie, and she looked up at the roof, where once again the hamster was sleeping, safe in his cage with the door tight shut. "How did you know about Ra..."

"La la la!" sang Nan with her fingers in her ears.

"We camped!" said Lulu. "In the garden all night! Mellie and I had cushions to sleep on. Nan had her crown and she sat on her throne."

"On her throne? *In the garden? But* WHY?"

Lulu took a deep breath. Then she bravely began.

"Well, you know Emma Pond..."

But Nan interrupted.

"Because it's my birthday!" she said.

# Look for more *Lulu* adventures!

**Lulu and the
Duck in the Park**
HC 978-0-8075-4808-0
PB 978-0-8075-4809-7

**Lulu and the
Dog from the Sea**
HC 978-0-8075-4820-2
PB 978-0-8075-4821-9

**Lulu and the
Cat in the Bag**
HC 978-0-8075-4804-2
PB 978-0-8075-4805-9

**Lulu and the
Rabbit Next Door**
HC 978-0-8075-4816-5
PB 978-0-8075-4817-2

**Lulu and the
Hedgehog in
the Rain**
HC 978-0-8075-4812-7
PB 978-0-8075-4813-4